Summer
Business

by Charles E. Martin

Greenwillow Books, New York

Library of Congress Cataloging in Publication Data
Martin, Charles E., (date)   Summer business.
Summary: By running small businesses catering to
the summer visitors to their island home, Heather
and her friends earn enough money for a trip
to the Harvest Fair on the mainland.
[1. Business enterprises—Fiction.
2. Moneymaking projects—Fiction.
3. Summer employment—Fiction.
4. Islands—Fiction.] I. Title.
PZ7.M356777Su 1984   [E]   83-25422
ISBN 0-688-03863-8
ISBN 0-688-03864-6 (lib. bdg.)

To small businesspersons
(under twelve),
wherever they may be

School was over. Visitors were coming to the island. "My father says everyone ought to learn how to work," Sam told his friends. "We should all work this summer." Everyone agreed.

But at the inn Sam was told he was too young.

"It's too late," they told Lulu at the store. "We have all the help we need."

At the library Miss Jackie told Heather she already had too many volunteers. "But," she said, "why don't you sell something? Get together and talk about it. You can use the picnic table on the back lawn as a meeting place. Ideas will come." Everybody had ideas.

They finally decided that Lulu and Hamilton would sell painted rocks and shells. Jonathan, May, and Sam would run a flea market. Kate and Heather would sell lemonade and cookies. Rita would dog-sit, pick up mail, and fill in wherever she was needed. She would also be treasurer. They decided they would save their earnings till the end of summer, except for what they spent on supplies—and occasional ice cream.

Getting ready was fun. They worked in Heather's father's fish house, painting stones and shells.

Kate's mother helped them bake cakes and make lemonade. Kate and Heather set up their stand close to the inn.

The first week everything was grand. The sun was bright and hot, though cold breezes hurt business twice. Heather's mother said not to be bothered, all businesses run into trouble from time to time.

ICE COLD
LEMONADE

May, Sam, and Jonathan set up the flea market on a stone wall. They had lots of lookers and some buyers. Sam's grandfather liked everything, until he saw the copper fish. "Now how could Becky have given you my old Tuna Tournament third prize?" he said. He took it back and next day brought them a brass-monkey pipe rack instead.

The painted rocks were displayed in front of the church. They sold so well the first week that Hamilton and Lulu worried about when they could help make more. They were too busy selling.

As Lulu's mother said, "There is no business without problems."

The flea market was such a success that Sam and Jonathan were beginning to worry about running out of things to sell. Sam's mother donated a few more objects, but there was one thing she refused to give away. Rita got so busy that she had to ask May to help her.

Then, suddenly, business turned bad. A heavy shower washed the paint off the rocks and shells. Lulu and Hamilton were stunned. "We used the wrong kind of paint," Hamilton said.

"Now we have nothing to sell," complained Lulu.

The next day Kate forgot to put sugar in the lemonade. A jogger came by and bought a cup. He coughed and sputtered. He told everybody about it and for a while nobody bought lemonade.

Hamilton was sitting in the family skiff worrying about what to do. A couple
on the beach asked him if it was possible to visit the ancient Indian rock drawings on
the small island in the harbor. Hamilton said he'd be glad to row them over.
They insisted on paying him. That gave him an idea
and he dashed off to find Lulu.

One Saturday and Sunday all business stopped. Everybody hunted for the Browns' cat. She had disappeared, and the Browns were coming back on the late boat Sunday. They searched the cliffs, both the beaches, through the woods, and under houses, but they did not find her. Then two hikers said they'd seen a cat on the White Head bluff. And sure enough, out of the darkness of Mermaid's Cave there poked a small yellow head. They passed the cat up from hand to hand and everyone was happy, especially the Browns.

A week of rain ruined the lemonade business. Kate went into full-time cat- and dog-sitting with Rita and May. Heather joined Hamilton and Lulu, who were very busy taking people to Indian Rock. Heather sold tickets and answered questions. Lulu stayed on the small island and escorted people to the site. Hamilton rowed people back and forth.

Rain, sun, fog, cold, or hot, they were always busy.

The flea market was almost sold out.
Business was dull. Sam's father said, "Why don't
you sell the old buoys? They're antiques. Everyone's
using plastic now. It's lighter. Get a wheelbarrow
and pick them up. I'll bet they'll sell." They did.
The flea market came to life again.

It was the second day of September. The passenger ferry came in empty and went away full. There had been almost no business anywhere for days. It was the first time they were all able to go swimming together.

"Before school starts, my mother wants to take me to the Harvest Fair on the mainland," Lulu said.

"I wish we could all go," Hamilton said.

"Why don't we use some of our money for the fair?" Heather asked.

Everyone thought it was a great idea. They would ask three mothers to take them. They would stay at a motel and spend almost two days at the fair. They all turned to Rita, the treasurer, who had been very quiet.

"I think we can do it," she said.

They saw a horse race. They entered and lost in the three-legged race. They won prizes. They bought things. They saw a strong man pull a wagon loaded with hay. They saw some lovely prize ducks, some huge prize pigs, prize chickens, cows, corn, and apples. They took all the rides. And when they reached the Crestwood Motel, there was nothing on their minds but sleep.

They crossed back to the island on a gentle sea. They talked about school. They talked about their earnings.

The next day they went to see Miss Jackie to tell her all about their trip.

"And," said Heather, "we even have some money left."

"What are you going to do with it?" asked Miss Jackie.

"Come with us and see!" said Rita. And they all left the library together.